United States Regions

West Coast Region

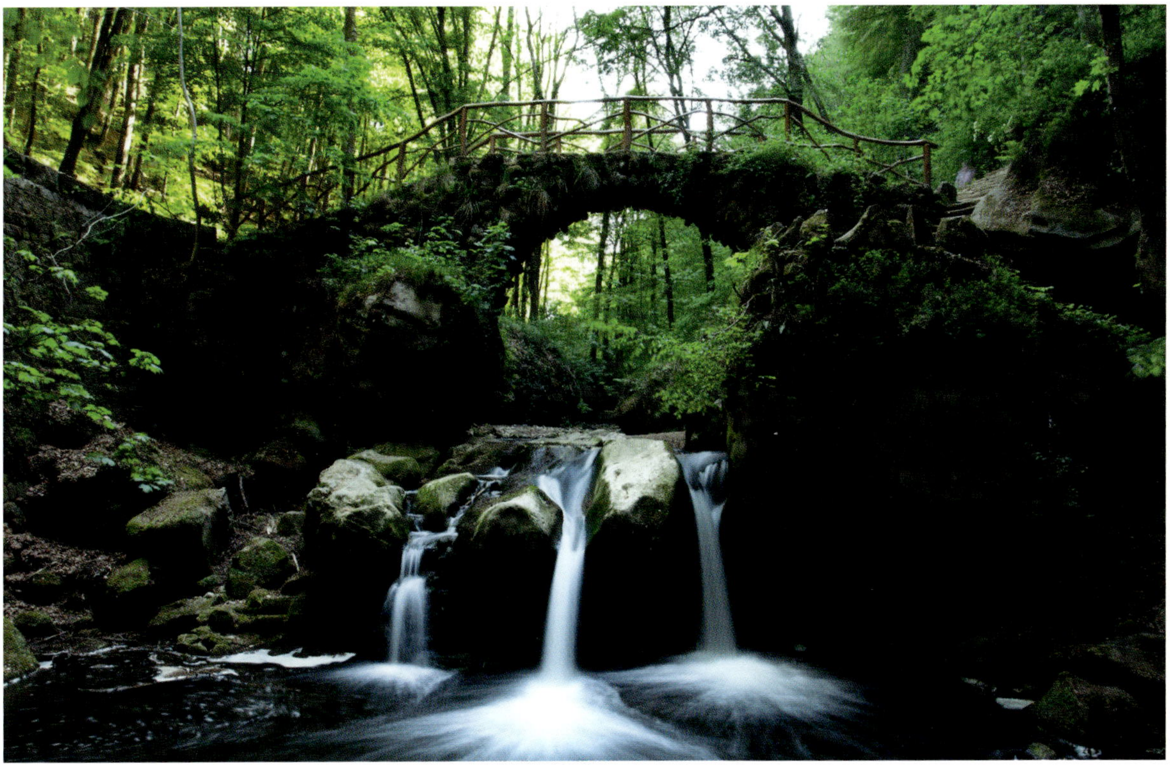

Sue Vander Hook

rourkeeducationalmedia.com

Scan for Related Titles and Teacher Resources

Before & After Reading Activities

Level: **Q** Word Count: **867 Words**
100th word: *nearly* page 6

Before Reading:

Building Academic Vocabulary and Background Knowledge

Before reading a book, it is important to tap into what your child or students already know about the topic. This will help them develop their vocabulary, increase their reading comprehension, and make connections across the curriculum.

1. Look at the cover of the book. What will this book be about?
2. What do you already know about the topic?
3. Let's study the Table of Contents. What will you learn about in the book's chapters?
4. What would you like to learn about this topic? Do you think you might learn about it from this book? Why or why not?
5. Use a reading journal to write about your knowledge of this topic. Record what you already know about the topic and what you hope to learn about the topic.
6. Read the book.
7. In your reading journal, record what you learned about the topic and your response to the book.
8. After reading the book complete the activities below.

Content Area Vocabulary
Read the list. What do these words mean?

active
diameter
endangered
migrate
missions
occasion
plentiful
port
prairies
rainforest
temperate
vegetation

After Reading:

Comprehension and Extension Activity

After reading the book, work on the following questions with your child or students in order to check their level of reading comprehension and content mastery.

1. Are loggers a good or bad influence on the environment? Explain. (Asking questions)
2. Do you currently have or use any products created by Apple, Microsoft, and Amazon? (Text to self connection)
3. In what ways were the first settlers on the West Coast brave? (Asking questions)
4. How would a species end up on the threatened and endangered species list? (Infer)
5. Why do animals migrate from one region to another rather than stay in one area? (Infer)

Extension Activity

Research a species that is on the threatened or endangered list. How did it get on the list? How long has it been on the list? Research ways you can help that animal. Create awareness posters for your animal. Suggest ways you can help get the animal off the list and keep it safe. Ask to put up the poster in your school or public library.

Table of Contents

The West Coast.......................4

Long Ago............................14

West Coast Jobs.....................18

What Are the People Like?...........21

Places to Visit.....................27

State Facts Sheet...................28

Glossary............................30

Index...............................31

Show What You Know..................31

Websites to Visit...................31

About the Author....................32

The West Coast

Can you imagine the tallest trees in the world? Now think about huge ocean waves. They crash over jagged rocks. Cold salt water flows into caves where sea lions live. Nearby are mountains and sandy beaches. This is the West Coast region of the United States. It stretches 1,500 miles (2,400 kilometers) along the Pacific Ocean.

The first section of State Route 1 in California was built in the 1930s.

A drive down the West Coast goes through Washington, Oregon, and California, and will take about four days.

In Washington, the coastline is a **rainforest**. The land looks like a jungle. It is covered with plants, moss, and large trees. Trees grow to nearly 300 feet (91 meters). That's almost as tall as the Statue of Liberty.

Further south into Oregon, the beaches become sandy and rocky. To the east are the mighty Cascade Mountains. Volcanoes are part of this rugged mountain range. Some are still **active**.

In the rainforest of Washington, snow stays in the treetops. It can't fall to the ground because the **vegetation** is too thick.

In 1980, Mount St. Helens in Washington erupted. This active volcano spewed out lava, ash, and rock. Ash fell on eleven states. Huge mudslides flowed 50 miles (80 kilometers) to the Columbia River. Fifty-seven people and thousands of animals died. It was the first volcanic eruption in the U.S. since 1915 when Mount Lassen in California erupted.

In Northern California is the Avenue of the Giants. The Redwood Forest is home to the largest and oldest trees in the world.

The tallest tree in the world is a Sequoia Redwood in California. It is 379 feet (115.5 meters) tall. The largest Redwood tree is 26 feet (7.9 meters) in **diameter.** That is the size of a large above-ground swimming pool. These trees can live up to 2,000 years.

Big Sur coastline

Steep mountains rise along the coastline south of the redwoods. The area is called Big Sur, which means, the Big South. The cliffs stretch 90 miles (145 kilometers) along the coast. Further south is Southern California. Large sandy beaches, palm trees, and sunshine make it a popular place to live or visit. Sometimes strong earthquakes shake the California land. Some of them have done a lot of damage.

Every year, gigantic whales **migrate** along the coast. Visitors come to see the whales. They also come to see hundreds of Steller sea lions that live near Florence, Oregon. They take shelter there in the largest sea cave in the world.

Walk along the beach and you may see crabs or sea stars in the sand. Look up into the sky and you may see a pelican, an osprey, or a gull. Plants and trees near the ocean grow where the air and water are salty. Some grow on rocky slopes. Strong sea winds batter them down.

Steller sea lions rest along the coast of Florence, Oregon.

Sea stars are a common site along the coastlines of California.

Conditions are better for plants and trees in the forests. They grow bigger and live longer. Animals are **plentiful** in the forest. It is home to black bears, deer, cougars, and mountain lions. Spotted owls and gray foxes live there. Bald eagles and hawks soar overhead. The huge Roosevelt Elk roam the forests and **prairies**.

Roosevelt Elk

Some of these animals are on the threatened and **endangered** species list. That means not many of them are still alive. It is against the law to hurt or kill them.

ATTENTION!

YOU ARE ENTERING PROPERTY DEDICATED TO THE STATE OF CALIFORNIA AS A WILDLIFE PRESERVE. THIS PRESERVE IS MANAGED FOR THE BENEFIT OF 31 ENDANGERED SPECIES. PLEASE HELP US TO CONSERVE THIS ENVIRONMENT BY RESPECTING THE PRESERVE. THANK YOU FOR YOUR COOPERATION.

TRESPASSING, DUMPING, AND MOTORIZED OFF-ROAD VEHICLES ARE STRICTLY PROHIBITED! VIOLATORS WILL BE REPORTED TO THE RIVERSIDE COUNTY SHERIFF'S OFFICE AND PROSECUTED. CPC 602;374(a)

PLEASE CONTACT WASTE MANAGEMENT, INC. AT (909)277-1740 FOR MORE INFORMATION ABOUT THIS PRESERVE, TO ARRANGE FOR A TOUR, OR TO OBTAIN A LIST OF LEGAL PLACES TO RIDE MOTORCYCLES IN CALIFORNIA.

American Bald Eagle

Long Ago

The West Coast region did not always belong to the United States. Native Americans lived along the Pacific Ocean. Then explorers came from Spain and Portugal. Others came from England and France. Many countries claimed this beautiful land was theirs.

It has been estimated that in 1492, one-third of all Native Americans in the United States were living in California.

Spanish explorers built **missions** and towns in California. The first mission was built in San Diego in 1769. There are now 21 Spanish missions in California. They are the oldest buildings there. The people who built the missions taught the Native Americans about Christianity. Some missions became schools. Often soldiers used the missions for a place to stay. Towns built up around these missions.

In 1805, Americans started settling on the West Coast. Americans fought with Mexico for the California land. Then in 1848, an American settler discovered gold. Thousands of people rushed to the West Coast in what was called the Gold Rush.

Ships brought people and supplies. People built railroads to get to the West Coast faster. The region changed rapidly. Cities grew on the coast. San Francisco became a busy **port**.

Railway workers lay track connecting the East and West coasts of the United States.

San Francisco

In 1911, a settler founded the first movie studio in Hollywood. Actors and musicians flocked to California. Walt Disney and others set up movie studios there. Disney built Disneyland. Tourists arrived to see Mickey Mouse and Donald Duck. The population of the West Coast grew rapidly.

West Coast Jobs

What kind of jobs do West Coast people have? Fishing is an important industry. Fishermen catch halibut and salmon from the ocean to sell. They trap shrimp, crabs, and clams. Large fish, such as tuna, swordfish, and shark, bring good prices at market. Many West Coast people work for technology companies. In California, many of them work in the Silicon Valley near San Francisco.

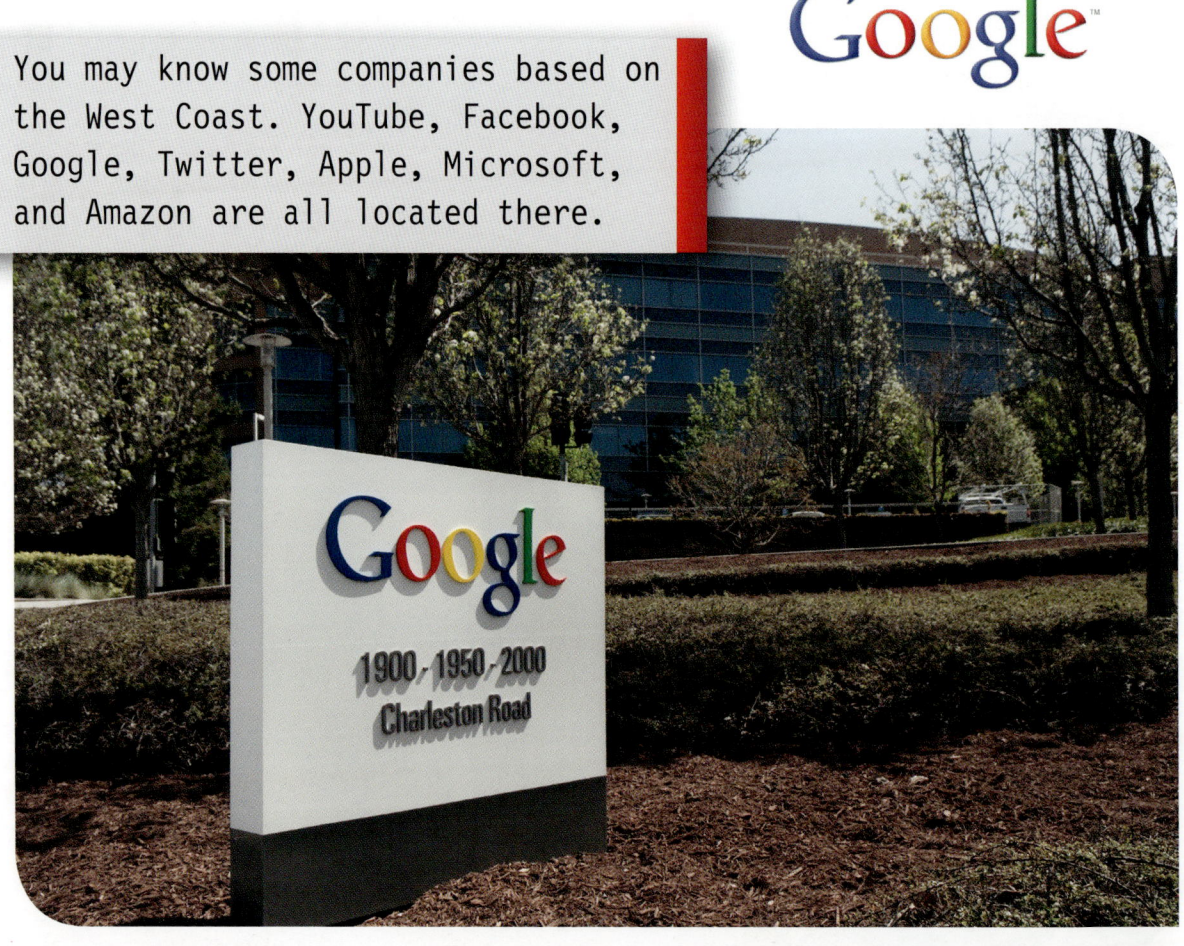

You may know some companies based on the West Coast. YouTube, Facebook, Google, Twitter, Apple, Microsoft, and Amazon are all located there.

In Washington, many people are loggers. They cut down trees and sell the lumber for houses. Some are farmers who grow apples and cherries.

In Oregon, the most important crop is flowers. They also grow hay, wheat, and onions. More Christmas trees are grown in Oregon than any other state.

Loggers often plant new trees to replace ones they have cut down.

California grows nearly half of all U.S. fruits, vegetables, and nuts.

In California, farmers grow more fruits and vegetables than any other state. Some of the crops are lettuce, onions, tomatoes, and carrots. Oranges and grapes grow well in the **temperate** climate. Some of the grapes become wine.

What Are the People Like?

The first settlers on the West Coast were brave. Many traveled on the Oregon Trail to get there. They came in covered wagons and crossed rugged mountains. They hunted for food.

Pioneers used covered wagons to carry their supplies.

Today, West Coast people are still risk takers. They have many new ideas and start interesting businesses. The beautiful weather attracts people to the region. They enjoy sunny beaches. Some like to surf when the waves are big. Others ski or mountain climb. Lakes, rivers, and forests are great vacation spots.

People dress casually in this mild climate. Jeans and T-shirts are often just right for any **occasion**. A hoodie can take the place of a jacket or coat.

Joshua Tree National Park in Southern California is one of the most popular rock climbing areas in the world. Over one million people visit Joshua Tree each year, many of them rock climbers.

People in California eat more seafood than the national average.

Food on the West Coast is usually fresh. Many people have their own vegetable gardens. Some grow orange trees and avocado trees in their backyards. Fruit is plentiful. Fresh fish is popular. Seafood restaurants and crab shacks on the coast serve fresh fish caught right there. People enjoy a healthy lifestyle on the West Coast.

West Coast people love their beautiful land. They care about their huge trees and sandy beaches. They protect their ocean, mountains, farmland, and animals.

Dungeness Crab Sandwich Recipe

Ingredients:

1/4 cup mayonnaise

3 ounces cream cheese

1 tablespoon chopped green onion

1 tablespoon chopped celery

1 teaspoon lemon juice

1/2 teaspoon Dijon mustard

Salt and pepper

6 ounces Dungeness crab meat

Directions:

Mix all ingredients together. Place crab mixture on toasted English muffins. Top with freshly grated parmesan cheese. Place under a broiler until brown and bubbly.

Crabbing along the Oregon coast is easy. Attach a rope to a crab trap and put some raw chicken in it. Lower the trap into the water. In about ten minutes, pull up the trap. There will probably be a crab inside. Boil the crab in water and eat it for dinner.

Places to Visit

- Olympic National Park in Washington: Visit the ocean, mountains, and rainforest. Explore more than 1,450 types of plants.

- Sea Lion Caves in Florence, Oregon: View sea lions in their natural habitat. Ride an elevator 208 feet (63 meters) down to see America's largest sea lion cave.

- Oregon Dunes National Recreation Area in Reedsport, Oregon: Ride off-highway vehicles on miles of shifting sand dunes. Go horseback riding on the beach.

- Redwood National Park: See the tallest, largest trees on Earth.

- Golden Gate Bridge in San Francisco, California: Walk or drive across one of the longest bridges in the world. It connects San Francisco to nearby Marin County.

- Hearst Castle in San Simeon, California: Tour what used to be the home of William Randolph Hearst. He owned the largest group of newspapers in the United States.

- Disneyland in Anaheim, California: Enjoy the large theme park created by Walt Disney.

- Mission San Diego de Alcalá in San Diego, California: Visit the first mission in California, now an active Catholic church.

State Facts Sheet

Washington
Motto: Bye and Bye.
Nickname: The Evergreen State
Capital: Olympia
Known for: Apples, Mt. St. Helens, the Space Needle
Fun Fact: The world's largest building, a Boeing assembly plant, is located in Everett, Washington.

Oregon
Motto: She Flies With Her Own Wings.
Nickname: The Beaver State
Capital: Salem
Known for: Crater Lake, Tillamook Cheese, Sand Dunes
Fun Fact: Oregon has more ghost towns than any other state.

California

Motto: Eureka...I Have Found It!
Nickname: The Golden State
Capital: Sacramento
Known for: Hollywood, Beaches, Wine Country, Golden Gate Bridge
Fun Fact: In California, Death Valley is the hottest, driest place in the U.S. It reaches 115° F (46° C) in summer.

Glossary

active (AK-tiv): an erupting or likely to erupt volcano

diameter (dye-AM-i-tur): the distance across a circle

endangered (en-DAYN-jurd): animals that people cannot hunt or capture

migrate (MYE-grate): to move from one region to another

missions (MISH-uhns): buildings used as churches

occasion (un-KAY-zhuhn): a special event or celebration

plentiful (PLEN-ti-fuhl): available in large amounts

port (port): a harbor for boats and ships

prairies (PRAIR-eez): areas of large grassland without trees

rainforest (RAYN-FOR-ist): a thick forest that gets a lot of rain

temperate (TEM-pur-it): mild; not too hot or too cold

vegetation (vej-i-TAY-shuhn): the plant life of a region

Index

beach(es)   4, 6, 9, 10, 22, 25
Big Sur   9
Cascade Mountains   6
crops   20
Disneyland   17
fishing   18
food   21, 25
Gold Rush   16
loggers   19
mountain(s)   4, 6, 9, 21, 22, 25
Native Americans   14, 15
ocean   4, 10, 14, 18, 25
rainforest   6
San Diego   15
Sequoia Redwood   8

Show What You Know

1. Where in California is the Hearst Castle located?
2. How do people on the West Coast dress?
3. What are some of the most plentiful crops grown on the West Coast?
4. What are some of the technology companies located in the Silicon Valley of California?
5. Who were the first-known inhabitants of the West Coast Region?

Websites to Visit

www.ca.gov/HomeFamily/ChildrenFamilies/JustForKids
www.oregon.gov/Pages/kids_corner.aspx
www.del.wa.gov/kids/wafunfacts.aspx

Author

Sue Vander Hook writes geography and history books for children. She grew up on the West Coast in Southern California. Her favorite pastime is taking road trips throughout the United States.

© 2015 Rourke Educational Media

All rights reserved. No part of this book may be reproduced or utilized in any form or by any means, electronic or mechanical including photocopying, recording, or by any information storage and retrieval system without permission in writing from the publisher.

www.rourkeeducationalmedia.com

PHOTO CREDITS: cover © photoquest7, biffspandex, IMNATURE, mkmaking photos, CampPhoto; title page © heringsroad; page 3 © Grace Butler; page 5 © Andrew Bayda; page 6 © Brandon Jennings, dave logan; page 7 © DaveAlan; page 8 © petrenkoua; page 9 © Paul Giamou 2010, olling, Sebastian_B; page 10 © Captain_Seabrine; page 11 © Yevgen Timashov; page 12 ©12 © bary mass; page 13 © Walter Spina, Rhea Margo; page 14 © Library of Congress; page 15 © tt4n; page 17 © Scotts Bluff National Monument, William Fawcett; page 18 © Eliza Snow; page 19 © Dmitry Kalinovsky, Dzainis Miraniuk; page 20 © StockRocket; page 22 © Elerium; page 23 m© Tom Grundy; page 24 © liv friis-larsen; page 25 © Jason Doly Photography; page 26 © pkripper503; page 28 © photoquest7, kwiktor; page 29 © oversnap

Edited by: Jill Sherman

Cover design by: Jen Thomas
Interior design by: Rhea Magaro

Library of Congress PCN Data

West Coast Region / Sue Vander Hook
 (United States Regions)
  ISBN 978-1-62717-667-5 (hard cover)
  ISBN 978-1-62717-789-4 (soft cover)
  ISBN 978-1-62717-906-5 (e-Book)
Library of Congress Control Number: 2014934375

Printed in the United States of America, North Mankato, Minnesota